Walt Disney's

Detective Mickey Mouse

A GOLDEN BOOK • NEW YORK

Western Publishing Company, Inc., Racine, Wisconsin 53404

Detective Mickey Mouse sat in his office, reading mystery
stories and waiting for a case.

"Gee, Pluto," Mickey sighed. "Maybe someday there'll
be a book about me—*Mickey Mouse in the Case of the...*"

Suddenly there was a knock at the door. Mickey
could see a shadow on the other side of the frosted glass.
"I wonder who that can be," Mickey muttered.

The door opened slowly. The visitor stepped inside.

"Why, you're the famous actress Lola LaWow!" Mickey exclaimed.

"How sweet of you to recognize me," the actress said. "I've come to you because Tutu, my dear sweet poodle, is missing. You must help me find her."

"She was last seen at my mansion, around breakfast time," Ms. LaWow went on. "Where, oh, where can she be?"

"We'd better go look for clues," Mickey said. "Pluto, you stay here and guard the office."

But Pluto was eager to go along and help search for Tutu.

Minnie Mouse was watering her garden when she noticed a fancy car coming down the street.

"Why, there go Mickey and Pluto and...Lola LaWow! Humph!" Minnie thought. "I wonder where they're going in her big fancy car."

Minnie decided to follow and see.

A few blocks from the mansion, Pluto suddenly started barking and trying to jump out of the car.

"Pluto, sit!" Mickey commanded. "Heh, heh," he chuckled, turning to Ms. LaWow. "I don't know what's gotten into him."

Meanwhile, Minnie stopped to read a big sign at the side of the road. It said, "Sassy Sausage Factory—Grand Opening Today!"

"Mmm, those sausages smell good!" Minnie said to herself.

At the mansion, Mickey said, "I'd better talk to all the servants. One of them may have dognapped Tutu."

"But everyone loves Tutu," Ms. LaWow said. "No one would…"

"Detective Mickey Mouse is on this case," said Mickey. "Bring in the first suspect."

In came Peeves, the butler. "The last time I saw her," he said, "Tutu was right by this door, whining and scratching to go out. But I don't have time to walk her *and* clean up the mud she tracks all over the house."

"Aha," thought Mickey. "He doesn't like cleaning up after Tutu. I bet the butler did it, just like in *The Case of the Missing Mongrel*."

Minnie was listening at the window. "Hmm," she thought. "Tutu must like the outdoors."

Next Mickey wanted to question the chauffeur. The beautiful actress led the way to the garage, and Mickey followed. Minnie secretly followed, too.

Inside, the chauffeur complained. "Walking Tutu is no picnic," he said. "Whenever we pass a butcher shop or a hot-dog stand, that little dog pulls at the leash till I stop and buy her a treat."

"This is just like *Puzzle of the Parked Cars*," Mickey decided. "It wasn't the butler. The chauffeur dognapped Tutu because he didn't like walking her."

But Minnie thought, "Gee, Tutu must really like meat."

"You can see the cook next," said Ms. LaWow. "This way to the kitchen."

The cook told Mickey that she was tired of preparing fancy dishes for Tutu. "All she ever wants are the sausages on Madame's breakfast tray," the cook sighed. "Tutu almost knocked me down this morning jumping for Madame's sausages. I had to carry the tray way up over my head."

"In *Mystery of the Merry Mousse*, the cook committed the crime," Mickey thought.

"That's the answer," Minnie thought quickly. "Tutu is crazy about sausages, and she didn't get any this morning."

"All this is too much for me," Ms. LaWow said, dabbing her eyes with her handkerchief. "I must rest now. I'll trust you to find the gardener yourself." She turned and went upstairs.

Mickey walked out the door into the garden.

"Hey, watch out!" the gardener shouted. "That's just what that little dog did—trampled all over my beautiful flowers!"

"So," Mickey thought, "the gardener is angry at
Tutu, too. They're all in this together. It's just like my
favorite story, *Case of the Kooky Kidnappers*."

Just then, Pluto sniffed the air excitedly and bolted
off through the flower bed.

"Not again!" the gardener moaned.

"Pluto! Pluto, come back!" Mickey called after the disappearing dog. "Where is he running off to? Now I've got *two* dogs to look for!"

"I bet I know where to find both dogs," Minnie said, popping up from behind a bush.

"Minnie! What are you doing here?" Mickey asked.

"Solving the case," Minnie replied. "Someone has to, while you're busy flirting with that actress."

"Oh, Minnie. You know you're the only girl for me," Mickey said.

Minnie smiled and grabbed Mickey's hand. "Okay. Let's go find those dogs!"

"If I'm right," Minnie began, "this small set of paw prints belongs to Tutu, and these larger ones are Pluto's."

Minnie and Mickey followed the trail. Soon Minnie sniffed the air. "Aha," she said. "Sausages."

They saw before them the new Sassy Sausage
Factory. A big crowd was gathered for the grand opening.
Suddenly everyone burst into applause. Minnie and
Mickey ran to see what the excitement was about.

"Why, it's Pluto!" Mickey exclaimed proudly.

"And that must be Tutu!" Minnie shouted gleefully.

The two dogs were doing funny tricks, and the manager of the factory rewarded them with fresh, plump sausages.

Mickey telephoned Ms. LaWow. "Your worries are over," he told her. "We've found Tutu."

After a big sausage lunch, Mickey, Minnie, and Pluto went back to the office to wait for another case.

"Now they want Tutu to be in the television commercials for Sassy Sausages," Minnie said. "She'll be a star, too!"

"I'm glad Tutu found a job. But I couldn't have found Tutu without you two," Mickey told his friends as he repainted the office door.